First Edition
Paperback ISBN: 978-1-62395-713-1
Hardcover ISBN: 978-1534-1059-8
eISBN: 978-1-62395-712-4
Published in the United States by Xist Publishing
www.xistpublishing.com
PO Box 61593 Irvine, CA 92602

First Edition
Paperback ISBN: 978-1-62395-713-1
Hardcover ISBN: 978-1534-1059-8
eISBN: 978-1-62395-712-4
Published in the United States by Xist Publishing
www.xistpublishing.com
PO Box 61593 Irvine, CA 92602

Merry Christmas Little Hoo!

Dedicated
to all the little
munchkins
in my life.

Brenda Ponnay

Scritch scritch scritch...scritch

What's that noise, Little Hoo?

Is it reindeer walking in the snow?

Scritch scritch scritch...scritch

No, Little Hoo.
It's just a branch
scratching on the window.

Jinga-ling jingaling, jinga-ling...

What's that noise, Little Hoo?

Jinga-ling jingaling, jinga-lin

Could it be bells ringing
on Santa's sleigh?

Jinga-ling jingaling

No, Little Hoo.
It's just White Cat
running in the snow.

Scuffle scuffle...scuffle scuffle...

What's that noise,
Little Hoo?

Scuffle scuffle...scuffle scuffle...

Is it Elves rummaging
in the kitchen?

Sorry, Little Hoo.
It's just a Mama Hoo
putting away leftovers.

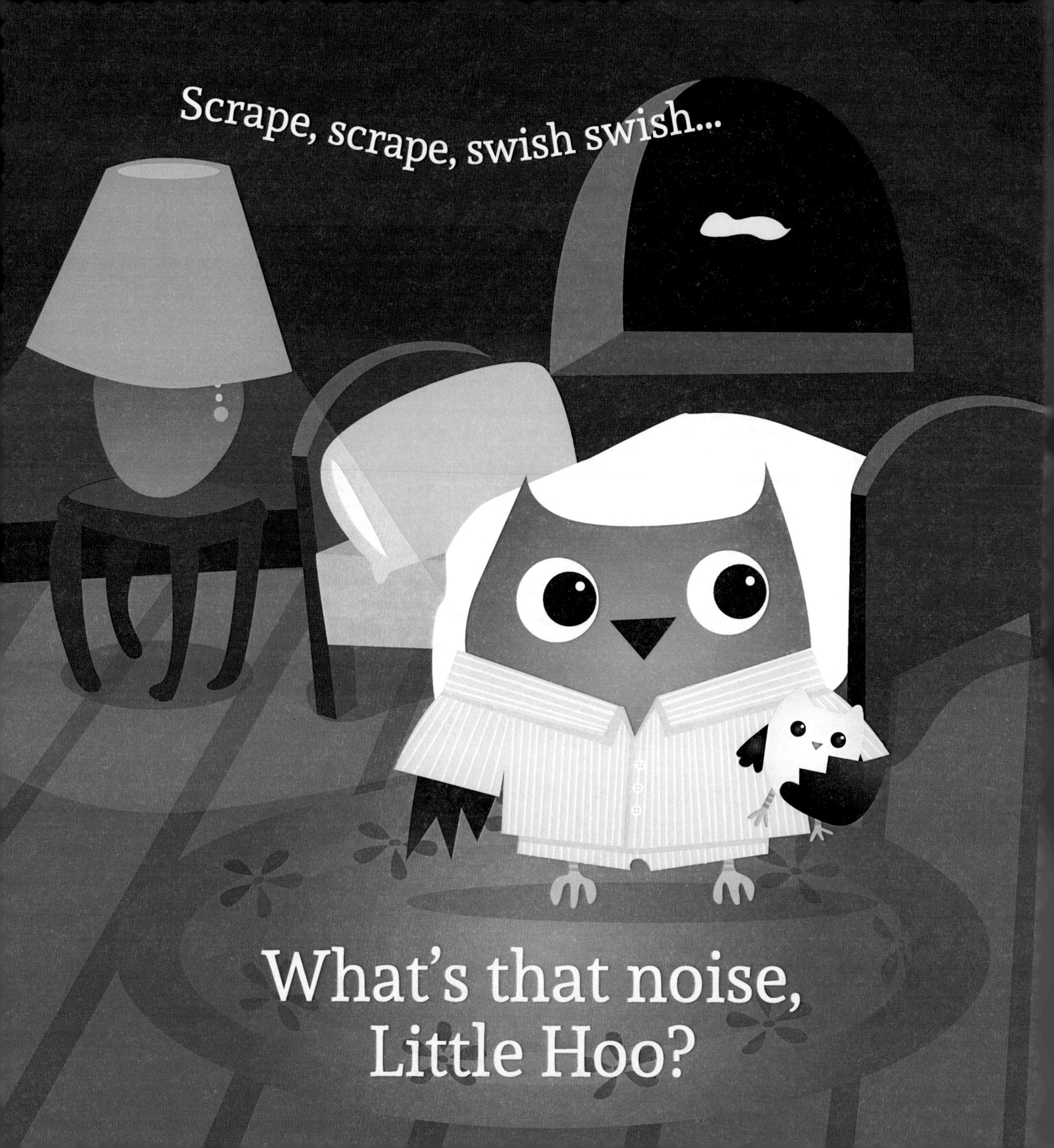

Scrape, scrape, swish swish...

What's that noise,
Little Hoo?

Is it Santa coming
down the chimney?

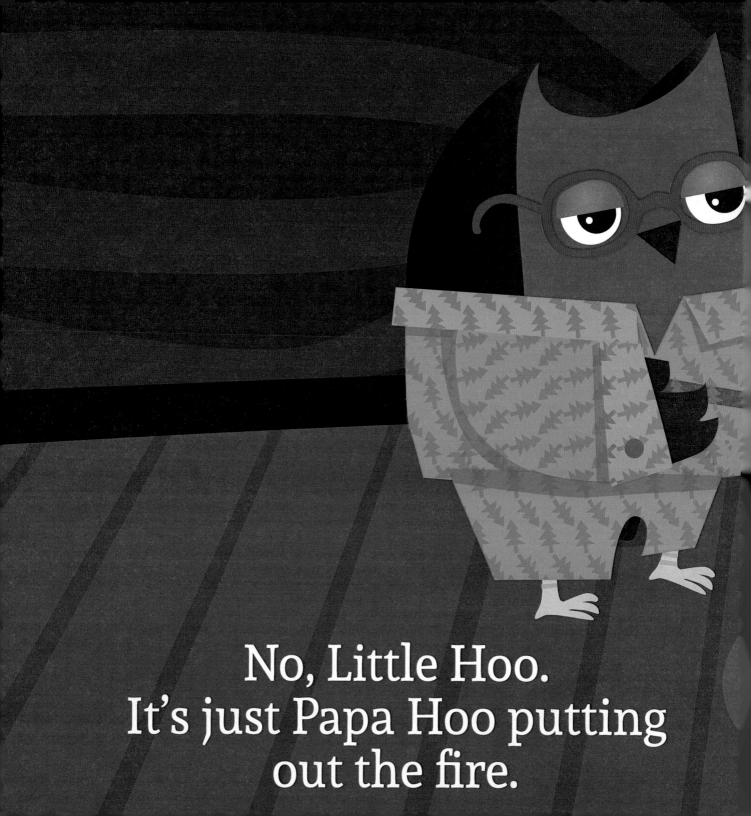

No, Little Hoo.
It's just Papa Hoo putting
out the fire.

Scrape, scrape, swish swish...

Munch munch, munch munch...

What's that noise,
Little Hoo?

ould it be a reindeer
unching on cookies?

Go back to bed,
Little Hoo.

ZZZZZZZ...... ZZZZZZZ

What's that noise?

ZZZZZZZ... ZZZZZZ...ZZZZZZZ...

It's Little Hoo sleeping!
Goodnight, Little Hoo.

Merry Christmas, Little Hoo.

Love Little Hoo?
Don't Miss the Other Books!

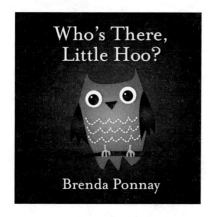
Who's There, Little Hoo? — Brenda Ponnay

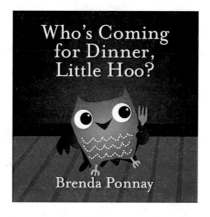
Who's Coming for Dinner, Little Hoo? — Brenda Ponnay

Little Hoo Goes to School — Brenda Ponnay

BE MINE — BRENDA PONNAY

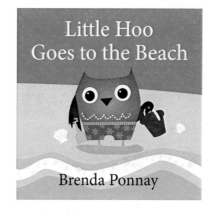
Little Hoo Goes to the Beach — Brenda Ponnay

Happy Birthday, Little Hoo! — Brenda Ponnay